BABAR
and the Runaway Egg

Harry N. Abrams, Inc., Publishers

One beautiful spring day, Babar and his children took a walk through the countryside.

"Spring is my favorite time of the year," Babar told them. "Look at the new leaves on the trees."

"They're such a pretty green color," said Flora.

"And look at these new flowers," said Babar. "They are daffodils."

"Look!" said Pom. "There's a baby deer with its mother."
"Many baby animals are born in the spring," said Babar.

"That bird is sitting on a nest!" Isabelle said.

"Yes, that is a mother bird keeping her eggs warm," said Babar.
"Maybe they'll hatch soon."

"Uh-oh," said Isabelle. "Look! That egg is getting away!"

Sure enough, one of the eggs had jumped out of the nest and was running down the hill.

"Runaway egg!" Pom cried.

The mother bird jumped off her nest and began chasing the egg, and Babar and the children joined in behind her.

   Up hill and down dale they went. They chased the egg past the art museum. "Catch it!" Babar called to the elephants who were nearby. But the egg was too fast for them.

They ran past the playground, but the egg did not slow down.

They ran past the palace, but the egg did not slow down.

Finally, the egg came to a stop all by itself.

"Listen!" said Flora. "What's that sound?"
"Tap-tap-tap. Crack!" went the egg. "Cra-a-ck. Cra-a-a-ck!"

A tiny head popped out of the egg. And then a little bird jumped out.

"Hello, little bird!" said Alexander.

The baby bird hopped over to its mother.

"Peep!" said the little bird.

"Squawk!" said its mother.

The mother and her runaway baby went back to the nest.
"Good-bye, little bird!" said the children.

"Spring is my favorite time of the year, too," said Isabelle. "It's full of adventures!"

Designer: Celina Carvalho

Library of Congress Cataloging-in-Publication Data

Brunhoff, Laurent de, 1925–
Babar and the runaway egg / Laurent de Brunhoff.
p. cm.
Summary: While Babar is out for a walk with his children one fine spring
day, Isabelle spies an egg rolling out of a nest and the entire family,
plus mother bird, chases it through the town.
ISBN 0-8109-4838-9
[1. Spring—Fiction. 2. Elephants—Fiction. 3. Eggs—Fiction. 4.
Birds—Fiction.] I. Title.
PZ7.B82843Baah 2004
[E]—dc22
2003016752

Harry N. Abrams, Inc., 100 Fifth Avenue, New York, NY 10011
www.abramsbooks.com

Abrams is a subsidiary of

LA MARTINIÈRE
G R O U P E